Presented to

_____

on

_____

by

_____

Christmas Stories

from Grandma's Attic

Christmas Stories

*From
Grandma's
Attic*

ARLETA
RICHARDSON

Chariot Books™
David C. Cook Publishing Co.

Chariot Books™ is an imprint of David C. Cook Publishing Co.
David C. Cook Publishing Co., Elgin, Illinois 60120
David C. Cook Publishing Co., Weston, Ontario
Nova Distribution Ltd., Torquay, England

CHRISTMAS STORIES FROM GRANDMA'S ATTIC
© 1991 by Arleta Richardson for the text and Kathy Kulin-Sandel for the illustrations.

Cover and internal design by Rick Schroeppel
Illustrations by Kathy Kulin-Sandel

First printing, 1991
Printed in the United States of America
95 94 93 92 91   1 2 3 4 5

Library of Congress Cataloging-in-Publication Data
Richardson, Arleta.
Christmas stories from grandma's attic / by Arleta Richardson.
     p.   cm.
"Chariot books."
Summary: Grandma Mabel relates the events of many past Christmases.
ISBN 1-55513-723-7
[1. Christmas—Fiction. 2. Family life—Fiction. 3. Christian life—Fiction.] I. Title.
PZ7.R3942Ch 1991
[Fic]—dc20
91-15755
CIP
AC

*To the wonderful people
who have worked over the years
to make the Grandma's Attic Series
so successful:*

• My editors, Cathy Davis and LoraBeth Norton;
*• Robert Thomas, who has typed and retyped,
and Phyllis Thomas,
who has faithfully proofread all these pages;*
*• and all the staff of the children's book division at
David C. Cook, who have been so helpful and caring
over the years.*
*I deeply appreciate all of you.
I could never have done it alone!*

Cranberries and Popcorn

*T*here is something comforting about the traditions of Christmas. Every year we are ready for carols, candles, bells, angels, and mistletoe. The tree decorations look new when they are unwrapped, even though some of them have been chewed on by three generations of babies.

We enjoy the same old stories, too. Just let someone say, "Marley was dead, to begin with. There was no doubt whatever about that," and there is no doubt that Charles Dickens is among us. Or hear, "And it came to pass in those days that a decree went out from Caesar Augustus . . . ," and we know that Luke is going to tell us the greatest story of all.

The human mind has a remarkable ability, both gratifying and horrifying, to relive a scene from years gone by, complete with sight, sound, and smell. Almost anyone you ask can come up with a story about a special Christmas. See how your mind zeroes in on the year you got a sled and there was no snow on Christmas Day? Or the year the tree tipped over? Or the year you didn't have a tree?

The Christmas stories in this book span the years from my grandmother's (Mabel O'Dell Williams of the Grandma's Attic Series) childhood to my own childhood. They cover the years when there was little material wealth with which to celebrate and the years when money was plentiful. But each story reflects a spirit that has nothing to do with poverty or plenty, and everything to do with love, joy, goodwill, and thankfulness. It is my hope that reading these stories will inspire you to go back and remember the cranberries and popcorn on your own string of memories. Merry Christmas!

—Arleta Richardson, 1991

A Lesson from an Angel

"These ornaments always look new when we take them out, don't they, Grandma?" I said. "I forget what they look like every year."

"Yes, they do," Grandma replied. "And some of them are older than you are."

We unwrapped the balls and celluloid animals and dolls and spread them out around the tree.

"This is my favorite," I said, picking up a little angel. "It's pretty old, isn't it?"

"Yes, it is." Grandma turned it over in her hand. "But it looks a lot better than another angel I remember. I wish I had saved it, even though you'd never know what it was, I'm afraid."

"What happened to it?" I asked. "Did you drop it?"

"Not exactly," Grandma said. "It was the victim of another one of our foolish tricks."

I was anxious to hear about it, so Grandma told me the story while we worked.

After what seemed like weeks of waiting, it was finally time to decorate the tree at school. Each class made something to hang, and there was a lot of competition for the prettiest or most unusual addition each year. This Christmas Miss Gibson had a surprise as her contribution to the festivities. She brought a box out of her desk.

"We're going to have an angel at the top of our tree," she announced, and she held up the most gorgeous ornament we had ever seen. "My aunt sent it for us to use, then I'll take it home with me." She placed it with the things we had made with the promise that we would start trimming the tree the first thing tomorrow. Everyone gathered around to admire the angel with its golden wings and halo, white frothy-looking dress, and outstretched arms.

"I can almost hear her singing 'Glory to God in the highest,' can't you?" Sarah Jane said. "That's the first thing everyone will see when they come for the program."

When we returned to our seats for the final minutes of the school day, Sarah Jane leaned over and whispered to me.

"I have a great idea."

"You always have," I whispered back. "I hope it doesn't have anything to do with me."

Miss Gibson assigned homework and dismissed the school. While we gathered up our books and put on boots and scarves, Sarah Jane revealed her plan.

"I don't think the angel should stay here in this cold building tonight," she said. "What if she freezes and cracks? Maybe we'd better take her home and keep her warm. We can come early in the morning before the others get here. Shall we ask Miss Gibson if we can do that?"

I agreed that this sounded like a good idea. We looked around for Miss Gibson, but she had been called out to settle a dispute in the school yard.

"I don't think she'll care," Sarah Jane said. "Here, I have a clean handkerchief to wrap the angel, and you can carry her in your lunch pail."

Something told me that we should wait and tell Miss Gibson, but she didn't return, so we packed the angel into the lunch pail and headed for home. I had been given permission to stop at Sarah Jane's to play after school, so we went straight to the Clarks' house.

"I'm glad you're home, girls," Mrs. Clark said. "It's getting colder. Mabel, your folks stopped by on the way to town and said that you should stay here until they get back. It may be after dark, so you'll have supper with us."

This was a pleasant surprise, and we hurried to take off our coats and run to Sarah Jane's room. We worked a few minutes on our homework, then played with her dolls until it was time to eat. Soon after supper, Pa and Ma arrived, and while they visited with the Clarks, I got my things together to go home.

"Where's my lunch pail?" I asked.

"I put it on the back of the stove," Mrs. Clark replied. "I thought we'd be sure to see it there when you were ready to head for home."

Sarah Jane and I looked at each other in horror, and as quickly as we could escape from the kitchen, we opened the pail. The sight that met our eyes was worse than we had imagined. The angel's face was crumpled, and her halo had melted to one side. Her arms were no longer outstretched, but lay at odd angles to her body.

"Oh!" I wailed. "This is the worst thing we've ever done. I didn't know she was made all of wax!"

Sarah Jane looked as stricken as I felt as we gazed at the ruined ornament.

"What do we do now?" she moaned. "Could we put it back and pretend we don't know what happened? No one saw us leave with it."

I shook my head. "We'd never sleep again as long as we lived," I said. "We'll have to tell our folks."

"And Miss Gibson," Sarah Jane added. She sat down on the bed. "I thought Christmas was supposed to be happy. This one sure won't be."

"We'll probably have to give up our presents to pay for it," I said. "This will be absolutely the worst Christmas we've ever had."

"Oh, my!" Mrs. Clark said when we broke the news to our folks. "I should have looked in that dinner pail before I put it on the stove. I had no idea there was anything like that in it!"

"I can't believe you'd do something so foolish," Ma said. "Or maybe I can. What are you going to do now?"

"We thought you'd tell us," I said. "We don't know."

"This is your problem," Pa told us. "You will need to talk to Miss Gibson about it. Find out how much it will cost to replace the angel, then decide how you will get the money."

"There's no way but to give up our Christmas presents," Sarah Jane said.

Mr. Clark nodded. "That sounds reasonable," he said. "It's a sorry fact that you pay for foolish mistakes."

"If we expected any sympathy, we can forget it," Sarah Jane said when we were back in her room.

"I expected something besides sympathy," I replied. "I'm surprised they didn't spank us, even if we are ten years old."

"I'd rather be spanked than have to face Miss Gibson in the

morning," Sarah Jane declared. "She is going to be so unhappy. We've ruined three Christmases."

We were in for another surprise the following morning when Miss Gibson looked thoughtfully at the ruined angel.

"I'm sure you meant well, girls. But we must learn to think things through before we act."

"How much do we owe you, Miss Gibson? Can you buy another angel for our tree?"

Miss Gibson was silent for a moment, then she shook her head. "We'll put this angel on the tree," she said. "It isn't as beautiful as it was, but maybe it will remind us that we can ruin anything if we don't consider the consequences of our actions. Perhaps we needed the lesson that things that can be broken are not as important as the love that came at Christmastime." She smiled and hugged us. "We'll tell the others that the angel had an accident, but she still stands for Christmas."

"In the dim light the angel still looked pretty," Grandma said, "but what we remembered most was Miss Gibson's wisdom in not putting too much value on things that could be replaced. We may not have been punished as severely as we should have been, but we did learn a good lesson."

The year I had diphtheria, we were quarantined during the Christmas holidays. My father brought things to us and left them on the porch and waved to me through the window. Mother and Grandma had to stay inside the house.

"This will certainly be a different Christmas," Mother said. "No shopping in the crowded stores, no wading in the snow."

"And no tree," I said. "No Santa Claus. And probably no presents."

Quarantined Christmas

"I wouldn't say that," Grandma put in. "Your father will see that you have a tree and presents. And you already have one good gift—you're getting well. Did I ever tell you about the Christmas we had diphtheria at our house?"

"What happened? Did you still celebrate?"

"Oh, my, yes. It wasn't just like all the other Christmases, but it was certainly special."

"Students," Miss Gibson said, "I know you are anxious to talk about the Christmas program, but we do have another half hour of classes. Let's pay attention to our books until dinnertime. This afternoon we'll assign parts for the program and draw names for gifts."

The room quieted for a time, but it was hard to concentrate on books. The girls in the fifth through eighth grades were eligible to be Mary, and there were only four of us this year. Miss Gibson put our names in a box, and a primary child picked one. That was the fairest way to decide, since all of us wanted the honor.

Sarah Jane poked me, then pointed to the row of seats near the window.

"Your brother has gone to sleep," she whispered. "How could anyone sleep when we're planning for Christmas?"

I thought this was odd, too, since Roy was never still long enough to sleep during the day, but I decided he had gotten too warm and dozed off. He didn't wake up when Miss Gibson announced that it was time to put our books away. My other brother, Reuben, was also watching Roy anxiously, but he was two rows away and couldn't nudge him.

I forgot all about anything else when Miss Gibson opened the paper handed to her and said, "This year, Mary will be played by Mabel O'Dell."

"This is the most exciting thing that has ever happened to me in school!" I said to Sarah Jane. "I can wear the blue robe and hold the baby Jesus. I wish the program were tonight."

"I'm glad it's you, Mabel," Sarah Jane said, "but you'll need to practice a few times. A week isn't long to wait."

When the noise of dinner pails and talking didn't arouse Roy, Reuben went over to shake him.

"Miss Gibson," he said, "I think Roy is sick. He's awfully hot, and he doesn't want to wake up."

Miss Gibson hurried over and put her hand on Roy's head.

"You'd better run home and get your father to come for him," she told Reuben. "He won't be able to walk that far, I'm afraid."

"I'd sure hate to get sick just before the Christmas program," I said to Sarah Jane. "I'll stay away from his room. Maybe Ma can have him cured before next Friday."

But when I arrived home in the afternoon, I found that this was not to be. Before I could tell Ma the good news about my part in the program, my world shattered.

"I'm glad you're home, Mabel," Ma said. "Are you feeling all right?"

"I'm fine, Ma. Wait till you hear . . . "

"It will have to wait, Mabel. I'm busy with Roy. The doctor has been here and says he has diphtheria. We all have to be quarantined."

"You mean we have to stay in the house?"

"We can leave the house, but not the farm," Ma replied. "We can't be with other people."

"But I have to be with other people for the Christmas program," I said. "We'll be able to go out by next Friday, won't we?"

Ma paused in her hurry around the kitchen and looked straight at me.

"Roy is seriously ill. We won't be able to go anywhere for the next three or four weeks."

I let this sink in for a moment. When the hopelessness of the situation really registered, I began to howl.

"But, Ma! I'm Mary! Don't you understand that I have to be there? What about my piece? They can't have a program without Mary! They can't get along without me!"

"I can, right this minute," Ma said grimly. "I know you're disappointed and would like some sympathy, but your brother needs me more. We'll talk about this later."

I ran to my room and threw myself onto the bed, sobbing wildly. As far as I was concerned, life was over. Not only would there be no school program, but there would be no church Christmas Eve service, no sleigh ride with the carolers, and no day to celebrate with the Clarks. Things were dark indeed.

Pa put his head in the door. "Mabel, Sarah Jane is waiting for you at the gate. You can stand a little way this side and talk to her, but don't go out."

I put on my coat and trudged down the lane to where she stood.

"Did you ever hear of anything worse than this?" I said. "How could Roy do this to me?"

"You don't think he did it on purpose, do you?" Sarah Jane asked.

"Well, no," I admitted. "It's not really his fault. But what will I do?"

"For one thing, you'll have two Christmases," Sarah Jane said. "The real day with just your family and another one with us when Roy is well. I know that doesn't help for the Christmas program, but you'll be back in time for the spring program. I'll stop by every day after school with your lessons so you won't get behind."

"I wish I'd gone home with you tonight," I said. "Then I wouldn't be quarantined here by myself."

"And not have Christmas with your folks? You wouldn't be able to stand that."

As I walked back to the house, I saw Pa and Reuben headed for the barn. Ma was lighting the lamps in the kitchen, and smoke curled up from the big fireplace chimney. I knew how the big room felt and how it smelled of good things cooking. I remembered how patient and comforting Ma had been when I was sick. Sarah Jane was right. What would Christmas be without my family? I was glad I didn't have to find out.

"I know Uncle Roy got better," I said, "but did you really have a nice Christmas that year?"

"Oh, yes," Grandma said. "Ma was busy, but she found time to bake cookies with me and to sew new doll clothes. Pa and Reuben played games with me, and we set up a little tree in Roy's room. It was a lovely Christmas, just as usual. It always is when you're with the people you love."

Christmas
Spirit

*M*a and I were returning from the barn, and we stopped to admire the white bushes and trees that surrounded us.

I shook the snow off the holly berries and sniffed the cold air appreciatively. "Aren't you glad you don't live where it's always cold or always hot?" I asked Ma.

"I suppose you could get used to anything," Ma replied. "But, yes, I'm always happy with a change of seasons. It wouldn't seem like Christmas to me without snow."

"I'll believe Christmas is here when the schoolhouse is decorated and the program ready," I said. "It's going to be so pretty this year. We're going out today to cut greens and find a

Mabel's account of her eighth grade Christmas, reprinted from Treasures from Grandma.

23

tree. This holly would look nice, too, wouldn't it?"

Ma agreed that it would. "Take the milk to the house, and I'll cut some holly for you," she offered.

I took the milk pail and started up the lane, when something occurred to me.

"I don't ever remember you handing me the milk pail without warning me not to spill it," I said. "Does this mean you think I'm a more dependable age now?"

Ma laughed. "It means you're at an age where you can clean up after yourself. You learn to be careful in a hurry when you have to mop the floor and wash your own clothes."

The morning at school dragged. Steam rose from the wet mittens arranged around the hot stove, and everyone who passed a frosted window had to put a wet finger on it to trace the pattern of ice.

"Isn't it almost noon?" Wesley asked. "We have too much Christmas spirit to pay attention to schoolwork."

"Oh?" said Miss Gibson. "Just what is 'Christmas spirit,' anyway?"

"Peace-on-earth-good-will-to-men," Sarah Jane answered glibly. "With maybe a little fun thrown in just for . . . the fun of it!"

"I understand your impatience," Miss Gibson admitted. "This is a special time of year, and it is fun. But I hope we can learn something about the true meaning of Christmas, too. Let's stop and eat now, and then we'll go look for a tree."

Everyone was in favor of that, and we ran to collect and open our lunch pails.

"Oh, dear," cried Belinda. "My sandwich is frozen!"

"We can fix that," Miss Gibson told her. "Unwrap your sandwich and lay it on the lid of your dinner pail, then we'll put that on the coal shovel and stick it in the stove. It will soon be toasty and warm."

That worked so well that the rest of us wanted to try it. "Mmm. Hot corn bread," Warren said. "This is almost as good as being home."

"And doesn't it smell just like a kitchen?" I put in. "There are a lot of things that cook on the stove all day. Why couldn't we have a hot dinner right here?"

"Soup is good," Sarah Jane chimed in. "It could simmer

away while we work."

"That sounds delightful," Miss Gibson agreed. "But how much work would we get done between sniffs?"

"Not much," we laughed. "It's hard enough now to wait for noontime."

Everyone finished eating in record time, and we were soon bundled up and ready to go. The woods behind the school always produced the most beautiful branches and a tree that was just the right size. Each class made decorations and tried to keep them a secret until the day came to hang them on the tree. Sarah Jane and I were the only eighth graders, and since Wesley was alone in the seventh grade, Miss Gibson suggested that he join us.

"I can see Wesley's contribution right now," Sarah Jane confided. "An apple with a bite out of it. Or a gingerbread man with a leg missing."

"You're probably right," I agreed. "He does like to eat. Maybe we can get him to carve a wooden cookie and paint it."

It was sheltered in the woods and didn't seem quite as cold. When we had gathered all the branches we could carry, we trudged back to the schoolhouse.

"We'll leave the tree and branches outside," Miss Gibson decided. "They dry out pretty fast in a warm room. Let's start working on ornaments, shall we?"

Just before dismissal time we drew names for presents. Each year Miss Gibson would put all our names in a box, and we would each bring a Christmas gift for the person whose name we drew. We weren't allowed to put a name back unless we picked our own.

"I hope I don't get your name," I said to Sarah Jane. "And I'd rather not have Warren Carter's, either."

"It's nice to be included in such intelligent company," she replied, "but I'm not exactly flattered."

"Oh, you know what I mean. I give you a present anyway. I don't want you to get mine, either."

On the way home Sarah Jane said, "Well, my present isn't going to be hard to fix. A big box of candy will do nicely."

"Wesley," I guessed.

"Right. I'll make some chocolate fudge and some divinity.

Whose name did you get?"

"Hannah's. I'd like to think of something to give her that would make her smile."

"You'll never do it," Sarah Jane said emphatically. "She has absolutely no Christmas spirit. Just hope she didn't get your name. I heard her say she wouldn't bring a gift if she didn't get a name she wanted."

"Want to trade with me?"

"No, thank you. At least Wesley can be depended upon to like what he gets, provided it stands still long enough for him to eat it."

"Do you think we ought to tell Miss Gibson about Hannah?" I asked. "We don't want the party to be ruined."

"I don't think Hannah would really do what she said," Sarah Jane replied. "She likes to complain, but she's not mean."

"I suppose you're right. Anyway, this is too nice a day to worry about it."

"There's a whole week of school until Christmas vacation," I said to Ma as we got supper. "I wonder if I can wait that long."

"I think it's possible," Ma replied. "Do you want to know how to make the time seem to go faster?"

"Oh, yes! How can I do that?"

"Plan to get more things done than you have time to finish," Ma said. "I know that works, because I've been doing it for years."

"I have plenty to work on," I said. "I have to finish Sarah Jane's gift and make something for Hannah, not to mention make Christmas presents for the family and get ready for the Christmas program."

"You won't have a problem waiting," Ma laughed. "That's already enough activity for two weeks."

Miss Gibson allowed us time to work on Christmas projects and overlooked the extra noise and restlessness. The decorations for the tree were better than they had ever been. Even the first graders' strings of cranberries and popcorn were longer and prettier.

"Wesley," Sarah Jane inquired one afternoon, "where are the rest of the candy canes for the tree?"

"I guess I ate a few," he confessed.

"A few! There are only two here, and we started out with ten! Now what do we do?"

"I'll get Ma to make some cookies to hang up," Wesley promised. "I'll bring them in the morning."

"If I believe that, I'd believe anything," Sarah Jane muttered. "You could eat a dozen cookies between your house and the road. I'll stop by and get them myself to be sure they get here."

"Honestly, Wesley," I said, "by the time you're ready to graduate, they'll have to roll you out of the schoolhouse."

Wesley grinned. "What would a growing boy be without an appetite?"

"I don't know," I replied. "I've never seen one."

The week did pass swiftly, as Ma had predicted. With her help, I made a pretty Christmas apron for Hannah. It was wrapped in green tissue paper and tied with red ribbon. The program was ready, too.

"The older pupils are putting on a play instead of reciting pieces," I told the family. "It's a Christmas story, but I can't tell you about it because it's a surprise."

"What are you, Santa Claus or one of the reindeer?" Reuben teased.

"That's not funny," I replied stiffly. "There is more to Christmas than Santa Claus. There's also a spirit of kindness and giving."

"Kindness we can use a lot more of," Pa remarked, looking at Reuben. "Suppose we show a little to the animals and bed them down for the night. Shall we, boys?"

"I'll be home at noon tomorrow," I told Ma as we did the dishes. "We have to be back at school early tomorrow evening to get everything ready for the program."

"I'm sure it will be just fine," Ma said. "I'm looking forward to it."

The program went off with hardly a mistake, and the time soon arrived for distributing the gifts. Wesley was chosen to hand them out as the names were called.

"He was born for that job," Sarah Jane whispered to me. "All he lacks is the beard and a red suit."

One by one the gaily wrapped presents were brought to their owner, who shook them and poked them to try to guess what might be inside.

"Mabel, yours must be clear at the bottom," Sarah Jane said.28

"Either that or Hannah got my name," I joked.

Finally there was just one gift left. The name on it was David Ross. He was sick and hadn't come to the program.

"You didn't get one!" Sarah Jane said in disbelief. "I didn't think she really meant it."

"And I gave her that pretty apron," I said. "See if I ever do anything nice for her again!"

The rest of the evening didn't seem quite so exciting to me, and I was glad when it was time to go home.

"It's not that I didn't get a present," I explained to Ma on the way home. "The worst part is that she embarrassed me in front of my friends! It just isn't fair. I wish I hadn't given her that apron."

"Do you give a gift just to get one in return?" Ma asked me quietly. "Is that what the spirit of kindness and giving is all about?"

"No, I guess it isn't," I answered. I was ashamed of myself for feeling as I did, but I was disappointed. It was hard to forgive Hannah for what she had done.

On Sunday I had a cold and stayed home from church. When the family returned, Pa came over to the couch where I lay and dropped a box wrapped in tissue paper beside me.

"This is yours," he said. "It's from David Ross. He had your name, but since he couldn't get to the program, his folks brought his gift to church today."

So Hannah hadn't gotten my name! I had wrongly accused her and been resentful about something that hadn't even happened.

"I was so sure I knew all about Christmas spirit," I told Sarah Jane later. "I feel awful for thinking such mean things about Hannah."

"You should," Sarah Jane replied. "After all, you know it's more blessed to give than to receive. And since you can use all the blessing you can get, you'd better be sure to give me a Christmas present!"

North Branch Gives Away Christmas

Mabel O'Dell moved to North Branch, Michigan, to teach school. There she met and married Len WIlliams, pastor of the small village church. Her lifelong friend Sarah Jane also settled in North Branch.

*T*he people of the little town of North Branch celebrated Christmas as they did everything else—together. The community had long ago outgrown the schoolhouse as a scene for festivities, and the town hall was decorated for the occasion. Sarah Jane and Mabel joined the other ladies as they cleaned the big room in preparation for the evening.

"I hear Zachary Burton has returned from Canada," Sarah Jane remarked. "Gladys is upset because he hired a farmhand while he was there. The man is on his way down now with all his worldly goods."

"That doesn't sound like such a tragedy," Mabel said. "Does Gladys think it's too close to the holidays?"

"I expect she's annoyed because he didn't consult with her before he did it," Sarah Jane replied. "I also expect we'll hear more than we want to know about the whole affair before it fades out."

She was so right. In the next few days Gladys made her rounds by sleigh and by telephone to express her displeasure.

"I told him he could have found someone right around here to work the farm. He didn't have to go way off up north to get a man."

"The men around here get logging jobs, Gladys," Mabel said to her. "You can't get anyone but a schoolboy to work on a farm."

"Zachary's been talking to you, too, huh?" Gladys snorted. "I could find a hired man if I set out to."

The week before Christmas, Mabel arrived early at Sarah Jane's to fill the bags of candy and nuts that would be handed out by Santa at the program, along with the gifts each family brought for exchange. Before she could shake the snow off her boots and remove her scarf, Mabel could see that Sarah Jane was bursting with news.

"I would have called you, but I wanted to see your face when I told you."

"What am I going to look like? Sad, happy, excited?" Mabel asked.

"Unbelieving and horrified," Sarah Jane chortled.

"You don't look too horrified," Mabel said. "What does this great news have to do with me?"

"Not just you. I think this will take in the whole town."

"Let's hear it," Mabel said with a sigh. "As long as I don't have to take care of it alone."

"The Burtons' hired man arrived last night."

"Is that all? We've been expecting him for days."

"Zachary didn't exactly reveal the whole story when he said he had a farmhand," Sarah Jane said. "The man brought a wife."

"Oh. Well, maybe she can help Gladys in the house. They have lots of room."

"Not that much," Sarah Jane declared. "They have eleven children."

"Eleven children! Sarah Jane, you are making this up!"

"And they don't speak English."

Mabel sat down at the table and stared at her friend.

"What, then?"

"French. And we all know how much French Gladys speaks. You look suitably horrified, all right."

"What is that poor woman doing?" Mabel gasped. "How is she feeding them? We've got to do something!"

"You're right," Sarah Jane said briskly. "Let's get this job done as fast as we can and make plans."

While Sarah Jane set pans of rolls to bake, Mabel called all the ladies she could reach.

"We need quilts, dishes, clothing, and food," she told them. "With that many children, you don't have to bother about sizes. Anything will fit someone."

"I know we have to go over there," Sarah Jane said, "but I want you to know that I'm not looking forward to it. We'll probably find that Zachary has had to move to the barn. What in the world will Gladys do with that many children?"

By the time the sleigh was loaded, Mabel and Sarah Jane had a pretty good collection from their two houses. They drove around to the back of the Burtons' and went into the kitchen, where they found Gladys standing at the stove, stirring a huge pot of cornmeal mush. She looked at them bleakly.

"Well, Gladys, how—"

"Don't even ask," she snapped.

"Where is everybody?" Sarah Jane ventured.

"Most of the children are out in the barn," Gladys replied. "And I sent that poor little wisp of a woman upstairs to lie down with the rest of 'em. She's been up since daylight scrubbing floors and clothes and young ones."

Gladys pushed the pot to the back of the stove and sat down.

"We'll find a place to store them all until the house out back is ready," she said. "What worries me is Christmas. Day after tomorrow is the tree celebration, and how are we going to get something for every child? They got here with the clothes on their backs and not much else. Zachary says they had to sell all their household goods to pay for the trip. We'll have to think of some way to find toys for them."

"We'll get on the telephone," Sarah Jane declared. "If we call everyone who will be at the Christmas program, we'll certainly get some ideas. And Gladys, the ladies will be bringing food and clothes over to help out."

The evening of the big program was cold and frosty, and people began arriving early for the festivities. The center of attraction as they entered the hall was the Christmas tree.

"Wow! That's got to be the biggest tree in Michigan!" a little boy exclaimed.

And indeed it may have been. The top brushed the ceiling of the building, and the branches filled the corner of the room. In addition to the decorations made by the children at school, each family had contributed something suitable to the occasion. Now as everyone came forward and placed red and green packages in the branches and around the bottom, the whole thing presented a sight to behold.

The Christmas story, complete with live animals surrounding the manger, was a program to remember. When the time came to distribute the gifts, Jerome Grayson, president of the school board, rose and faced the crowded room.

"You all know that a new family has arrived this week to be with the Burtons. Even though the Martines may not have understood all that was said tonight, they are going to understand what we do. To begin with, the students at the school have voted to give every gift on the tree to the Martine family. They don't want the children to be without presents their first Christmas here. Secondly, the board of trustees has organized an all-town work day for tomorrow. Everyone who can possibly do so will gather at the big house in the morning to get it ready for the Martines to move into before Christmas. We will make any necessary repairs, paint and scrub, and collect furniture from anyone who has something to spare. Any ladies who can provide dinner and supper for the workers will be welcome. If we have never felt the true spirit of Christmas before, we surely will this year."

"Jerome never spoke a truer word," Sarah Jane groaned as they sagged down in front of the fire the following evening. "Can you believe that those people are all moved in?"

"I can," Mabel said. "I can also believe that we are tuckered out. But wasn't it worth it to see the expressions on their faces when they realized that the house was really theirs? I'll never forget how those children looked when the men moved the big tree into the living room and put all the packages back on it."

"Gladys forgave Zachary for the shock when she found out that Charles Martine had lost his last job and his home in Quebec. They would have been out on the street if Zachary hadn't offered to bring them here. Gladys might make a lot of noise about it, but she would never turn away anyone who was homeless."

Sarah Jane rose and went to get her coat.

"I'm glad that tomorrow is a designated day of rest," she said. "And if I ever said that there was nothing to see or do in a small town, I take it back. I've just seen it and done it!"

A Different Christmas

$\mathcal{A}$side from a trip to visit Grandpa and Grandma Williams, Alma's first introduction to society was the school Christmas program. We arrived a little early, and my former students clustered about for a good look at the baby.

"Does she eat much?" Teddy Sawyer wanted to know.

"You can tell she doesn't," Toby Elliot answered for me. "You can barely see her nose." He looked at me anxiously. "I wasn't expecting anything this little. Does she even weigh a pound?"

"Oh, yes," I laughed. "She weighs almost seven pounds. She won't be this little for long, because she does eat a lot."

Mabel's account of the first Christmas after baby Alma was born. Adapted and reprinted from New Faces, New Friends.

"I'll be in seventh grade when she starts to school," Nancy Lawton said. "I'll watch out for her and help her with her work."

"Thank you, Nancy," I said. "It will make me feel better to know that someone responsible is looking after Alma."

Families began to arrive for the program, and the children disappeared behind the curtain that was stretched across the front of the room. Everyone stopped to see Alma and talk to me.

"You should have held an open house for the town before you ventured into a public program," Sarah Jane chuckled. "Alma's the only one not saying anything, and she's the hit of the show."

"Never mind," I said to my friend, who was expecting a baby shortly herself. "Your day is coming."

"It can't be too soon for me," she replied.

The program began with the manger scene. One by one the schoolchildren appeared with wrapped boxes representing God's gifts. A poem, a song, or a short essay identified each gift. Roseanna and Joanna, twin six year olds, held a big box between them and recited:

"God gave a double blessing,
This is what we say;
When He gave the moon to shine at night,
And the sun to shine by day."

Teddy Sawyer's box held the gift of education. Toby Elliot had the gift of peace, and Joel Gage had parents. Everyone had something appropriate to say about his present before he placed the box under the tree. The program concluded with a song by the whole school and the usual bags of candy and nuts.

Mary Webster, the new teacher who had taken my place, flushed with pleasure as the parents congratulated her on the children's success. "We worked together to write the speeches and the poems," she said, "but the ideas were all their own. We wanted to show the true spirit of Christmas in a different way."

"You certainly did that," Len told her. "The program was very well done."

"Nobody had the gift of snow," Daniel shouted from the doorway, "but we got it!"

We certainly did. The snow was falling in thick flakes as we hurriedly left the schoolhouse. Since we had all come in buggies, not sleighs, we were anxious to get home.

"I trust that this is a temporary gift," Sarah Jane sighed as we parted. "This is not the winter I want to be snowed in with no human fellowship."

With Christmas came another heavy snowstorm. I had a twinge of wishing that I had accepted Ma's offer to go back with her the week before.

"You could bring the baby and come home with me now," she had said. "Len could come before Christmas and spend a few days. Pa is anxious to see his granddaughter, too."

Len had urged me to do that, but I declined.

"It would be the worst Christmas ever if something happened so we couldn't celebrate together. I'll wait and go with you," I told him.

Now in spite of being lonesome for my family, I didn't regret my decision.

"It's only right that we begin our own Christmas traditions, now that we have a family," I said. "If there isn't a blizzard on Christmas Day, we can get out to visit our friends."

On Christmas Eve day, Len and Thomas, Sarah Jane's husband, went to the woods to get trees.

"I think we can trust them to get nicely shaped ones," Sarah Jane said. "I know right where I'll put mine—in front of the parlor window. Do you think we have enough ornaments for both trees?"

We looked over the array of small things that we had been making: little wreaths made of red and green yarn, crocheted white snowflakes, pine cones decorated with holly berries, and small sleds made with twig runners.

"That will be plenty when we've finished stringing popcorn and cranberries tonight. We have red bows to add if there's more space to fill."

"If I were in any shape to tramp around in the woods, Thomas wouldn't have gotten away without me," Sarah Jane said. "Next year the babies will be a year old, and we'll all go and pick out the trees."

A pot of soup bubbled on the back of the stove, and I made corn bread to go with it while Sarah Jane mixed the dough for an apple cobbler.

By the middle of the afternoon the sky was beginning to darken, and snow fell in little wisps.

"They'll be coming in soon," Sarah Jane said as she peered out the window. "They shouldn't have had any trouble finding something. In fact, here they come now."

I went to the window, and we watched silently as the sleigh turned in the lane and stopped in front of the gate. As far as we could see, there was absolutely nothing in the sleigh except Len and Thomas.

"Well, so much for a tree this year," Sarah Jane sighed. "We'll put wreaths on our ears and cranberries in our hair and be satisfied. I'm going to be interested in the story that goes with this trip."

I opened the door and the men came in, brushing the snow off their coats.

"Did you have fun playing in the snow?" I asked them. "Or did the two of you spend the day visiting with friends?"

"Why, no," Thomas replied. "We just came in to see where you wanted your tree before we lug it in."

"I hate to be the one to tell you this," Sarah Jane said, "but if you cut down a Christmas tree, you forgot to put it on the sleigh."

"Actually, we didn't cut it down," Len replied.

"I can see that," I told him. "I'll watch you 'lug it in' before I tell you where to put it."

"Whatever you say." Thomas shrugged, and they turned around and went back to the sleigh. Then they came carrying a small tub between them. It contained a perfectly shaped blue spruce about two feet tall.

"While we were walking through the woods, looking for trees with just the right shape, we saw a lot of saplings," Len explained. "They've been sheltered, so they're not all pushed out of shape. We thought that in honor of the babies' first Christmas, we'd have a tree that we could put inside, then plant out by the lane as a remembrance. If you're too disappointed, we still have time to get a couple that we marked."

"Disappointed?" Sarah Jane said. "I think it's a wonderful idea! We'll be able to watch them grow with the children. You couldn't have done better if we had been with you."

"That's a vote of confidence if I ever heard one!" Thomas laughed. "Do we get whatever smells good for our work?"

After Alma was fed and asleep, Len popped corn in the fireplace, and we made many strings of popcorn and cranberries.

"What are we going to do with all of this corn?" I wondered.

"I suggest some butter and salt on what's left over," Sarah Jane said.

"How about popcorn balls?" Len said. "We could take some to the Graysons' tomorrow." We had all been invited to our friends the Graysons' for Christmas dinner.

"Good! Let's make snowmen for the Grayson children!"

For the rest of the evening we tried to outdo each other with creative figures made from sticky popcorn. Thomas made a lamb, complete with currants for eyes. Sarah Jane made a pig that sported a curly yarn tail. Len won the prize with a sleigh, piled high with candy canes.

"Daniel will love that," I said. "And Serena's not too old to appreciate an animal or a snowman."

Christmas morning was cold and stormy. Len heated a soapstone for my feet and wrapped a heavy robe around Alma and me. I had already bundled the baby into a woolen bonnet and coat and several heavy blankets.

"I hope she doesn't smother in there," I said as we started out.

"She won't as long as you're holding her right side up," Len said.

I was sure that I was, but I unwrapped the layers enough to see her face anyway. The scarf around my face froze almost at once, and the snow clung to my eyelashes.

It took less than ten minutes to reach the Graysons', and Regal seemed to enjoy the trip more than anyone. He pranced and shook his head and snorted happily. When we drove into the yard, Daniel threw open the front door and the whole family hurried out to meet us.

"Oh, please, Mrs. Williams, may I carry the baby in?" Serena pleaded. "I promise I won't drop her."

"I doubt she'd feel it if you did, she's so well padded," I said with a laugh, and handed Alma to her. Len and Jerome took Regal to the stable, and the rest of us went into the house.

I drew in a deep breath. "Wait until Sarah Jane walks in," I said. "She'll sniff and say, 'Bayberry. I love bayberry candles. They smell like Christmas.' You just see if she doesn't."

Serena laid Alma on the sofa and pulled back the blankets.

"Are you sure you put the baby in here, Mrs. Williams? I haven't found her yet."

"She was there when I left home. Keep digging."

"Here they are!" Daniel shouted from his post at the window, and Alma awoke with a howl of protest.

"She's here, all right," Serena reported, and we unwrapped her as quickly as we could. After the coat and bonnet were removed, and Serena was seated in the rocker with her, Alma's cries subsided. She seemed to look around with interest.

"I think she can see the tree," Serena said as Sarah Jane walked in with Myra.

"Of course she can," Sarah Jane said. "And she can smell the bayberry candles. They smell like Christmas."

Myra laughed at the direct quotation as she took Sarah Jane's coat and scarf. "Good," she said. "I've made some for you to take home. I'm so glad you could all get here. Since you all have brothers and sisters for your parents to be with today, I don't feel sorry for any of them. Sit down, and I'll bring you something hot to drink."

The day rivaled anything that Dickens ever wrote about Christmas. We played games, sang carols, and admired Daniel's and Serena's gifts. They enjoyed their popcorn toys, and Myra had to be quite firm with Daniel to keep him from consuming several before dinnertime.

The meal that Myra put before us was a feast indeed. There were tender turkey and ham, fluffy mashed potatoes and candied sweet potatoes, creamed onions, peas and carrots, as well as hot rolls and butter, pickles, jam, coleslaw, and cranberry jelly.

"When Daniel was about three years old," Jerome said as he carved the meat, "he thought we weren't filling his plate fast enough, and he complained loudly.

" 'You must have patience, Daniel,' his mother told him.

" 'I don't want patience,' he replied. 'I want turkey!' "

Daniel grinned self-consciously as we all laughed.

"He's probably thinking the same thing right now," Serena observed. "Fortunately he's old enough not to say it."

The day ended too soon, and it was time to return home for the chores.

"This has been as different a Christmas as I've ever had," I said, "but one of the nicest I can remember. I thought I'd miss being with my family, but I really was with them. Family is wherever there are people you love."

I was searching through Grandma's old trunk for some pictures when I came across a small, leather-bound book, the edges crumbly and dusty. It was a copy of Snowbound, *and "John Greenleaf Whittier" was inscribed on the first page.*

"Look, Grandma," I said. "Is this the book you told me about that Sarah Jane signed?"

"No," Grandma replied. She turned the book over lovingly. "This is the original one."

"But you sold that one to Warren Carter."

"I did," Grandma nodded. "The money he gave me helped get a coat with a fur collar for Ma's Christmas."

"But, how—?"

"How does it happen to be here? That's quite a story," Grandma said. "I guess I've never told you more than the first part of it."

"Tell me now," I urged her, and together we went back in time to Mabel's high school years.

The Gift That Kept on Giving

$\mathcal{W}$arren Carter did give me five dollars for my autographed copy of *Snowbound,* and for four years I was content with the copy that Sarah Jane had signed to look like the original. Ma enjoyed her coat so much that I never regretted the choice I had made.

Just before we graduated from high school, Warren stopped in to see me one evening.

"Mabel," he said, "you've given me a run for my money ever since we started school together. I probably never would have studied so hard if you had been easier to beat. I think you deserve a graduation gift for making me work."

Arleta learns the sequel to Grandma's story "The Autograph," that was told in Treasures from Grandma.

He handed me a wrapped and ribboned package, and grinned happily as I opened it. It was the copy of *Snowbound* I had sold to him in the eighth grade. "Oh, Warren! Are you sure you want me to have this back?"

He nodded. "It's too valuable a thing for you ever to have sold. You've been a good friend over the years, and I want you to keep it."

The book went with me to my new home, and whenever I looked at it I thought of Warren's generosity. Then one Christmas, when Alma was about eight years old, there was no money for gifts for the family. Sarah Jane and I made doll clothes from scraps for our daughters' dolls.

"What are you doing for Len this year?" Sarah Jane asked as we worked on our sewing. "You haven't said anything about it."

"I've made him a sweater and socks," I said, "but the truth is, I want to get him a Bible. We have a nice family Bible, and the church Bible of course, but he needs a reading Bible the size of his hymnal. I could get one from the catalog for seventy-five cents, but it's bound in cloth. The one I really have my eye on is bound in French Morocco and has gold edges."

"How much is it?"

"$1.40. I pick it up and look at it every time I go into Gages' store. Maybe I'll give it so much wear that they'll lower the price."

"Dorcas would let you get it and pay a little at a time," Sarah Jane said. "In fact, she would insist, if she knew you wanted it."

I shook my head. "Len wouldn't enjoy reading it if he knew I'd gone into debt for it. He would say that a Bible here and one at the church is enough. But I know how much he'd like one he could carry with him."

"How much do you still need?"

"Seventy-five cents."

"More than you'll get for your eggs," Sarah Jane said. "What else could you sell?"

"Nothing that I know of." I shrugged. I thought for a moment. "Well, maybe there is. My autographed copy of *Snowbound.*"

Sarah Jane was appalled. "Oh, Mabel, no! I was thinking of

something to eat, like cream or vegetables. That book is priceless!"

"So is Len," I replied. "I'll take it in to Dorcas and see if she'll buy it. Or at least trade it for the Bible."

Sarah Jane wasn't convinced that this was a good idea, but she said no more. The next time I went into town, I took the slender volume and explained my plan to Dorcas Gage.

"Are you sure, Mabel?" she protested. "This book is a treasure. Mr. Whittier is dead now, and there may not be many autographed copies of one of his most famous poems."

"I know. But how often do I read it? Len would read his Bible every day."

Dorcas was reluctant, but she took the book in return for the Bible, and I hurried home, more than pleased with my bargain.

When gifts were opened on Christmas morning, Len was delighted, as I knew he would be. As usual, we shared the day with Thomas and Sarah Jane. As we prepared to leave their home that evening, Sarah Jane handed me a small package.

"One more little gift," she said.

When I opened the present, I very nearly burst into tears. It was my autographed copy of *Snowbound*.

"Who knows what that book might buy next year?" Sarah Jane said with a grin. "I figured this was the best investment you could ever have."

But she was mistaken. Actually, the best investment of my life had been her friendship.

The Acme Queen Parlor Organ

*I*t was a crisp December morning, and Sarah Jane and Mabel were preparing for a shopping trip in town. As the two friends stepped out of Sarah Jane's front door, Mabel shielded her eyes from the glare of the sun and looked toward the road.

"Sarah Jane, isn't that Hudson Curtis turning into the lane?"

Sarah Jane looked and agreed that it certainly appeared to be. They had not seen a lot of Hudson in North Branch since he and Widow Moore had married and settled down in Greenwood with her two small daughters. As minister of the Greenwood church, Hudson was presumably busy with his flock and his new home responsibilities.

"Why would he be coming here?" Sarah Jane wondered aloud. "You're the one he turns to in time of crisis."

"We're about to find out," Mabel replied, and they walked

over to meet him before he could alight from his sleigh.

"Good morning, Sarah Jane, Mabel," he said. "Lovely day, isn't it?"

"Beautiful," Sarah Jane agreed. "What brings you to town, Hudson?"

"Good morning, Hudson," Mabel quickly interjected. "How are Addie and the girls?"

"Fine. Just fine," he answered. "In fact, Addie is the reason I'm here."

They waited for him to continue.

"Christmas will be here soon," Hudson went on. "I made a mistake last year."

"No news there," Sarah Jane muttered under her breath.

"My folks never made much of Christmas," Hudson said. "They thought giving presents to people who didn't need them and probably didn't want them was a waste of time. If they wanted something, they bought it. So we never exchanged gifts. But, after not giving Addie anything for the past couple of years, I've finally realized that isn't her way. Not that she complained," he hastened to add. "I just sensed that she was disappointed. So this year, I decided to make it up to her. That's why I came to ask your help, Sarah Jane."

Sarah Jane blinked in surprise. "You want me to buy a Christmas present for Addie?" she asked.

"Oh, no. I've already decided what to get for her. Since you live closest to the station, I thought you might keep it in your parlor until Christmas."

"Closest to the station? You're buying her a train?"

As usual, the intended humor sailed right over Hudson's head.

"Oh, no. I'm getting an organ from Sears and Roebuck. And I don't want it left at the depot."

This seemed reasonable. "I guess we could keep it for a couple of weeks," Sarah Jane said. "That's a very nice gift, Hudson. Addie will enjoy it."

He nodded. "Yes, she has hinted that she would like the girls to have music lessons. I'll have it shipped in your name and ask Percy to bring it over here. I'm really much obliged to you, Sarah Jane. I'll come and get it the week before Christmas."

Thus was the stage set for a comedy of errors that would have satisfied even Shakespeare's sense of the ridiculous.

It didn't often happen that Sarah Jane's husband had to be away overnight on business, but when Jerome Grayson couldn't get free to make a trip east to interview new surveyors, he decided to send Thomas in his place. Thomas was to be gone until the week before Christmas.

"At least he won't be here to tease me about getting involved with Hudson's schemes," Sarah Jane said, telling Mabel about the intended trip. "The organ will have come and gone before he gets home."

A few days later, Percy and a helper came bearing a heavily crated object and brought it into Sarah Jane's parlor. It was addressed in large letters to "Mrs. Thomas Charles, North Branch, Michigan." It did take up a large amount of wall space.

"Jessica is disappointed," Sarah Jane said when Mabel stopped by to see the crate. "She fully expected to be able to play the organ until Hudson came to claim it. She's not convinced that we couldn't take off at least the front of the crate."

"I'd like to see it, too," Mabel replied. "But Hudson didn't say anything about opening it."

"No. That might not stop me, except that I know it will be easier to transport in a crate. We'll have to visit the Curtis home after Christmas."

The following week Mabel received a startling call from her friend.

"Mabel, you will not guess what stands in my parlor."

"I wouldn't even try. What is it?"

"I don't know."

"What do you mean, you don't know? Aren't you looking at it?"

"Yes," Sarah Jane admitted, "but I don't believe it. Come over and see."

"Well, what in the world?" Mabel said, gazing at a second crate identical to the first in the middle of Sarah Jane's parlor floor, and addressed to "Mrs. Thomas Charles, North Branch, Michigan."

"My words exactly," said Sarah Jane. "Percy just stood in the door and said, 'It come on the morning train, ma'am. I was told to bring it over, and here 'tis.' That was all he knew and all he wanted to know."

"I guess you should have told Hudson to park Addie's organ in his father's bank," Mabel said. "I hope they aren't going to keep coming from now until Christmas. Do you think he's getting one for his church?"

"More likely he forgot he ordered it and sent for another one," Sarah Jane said. "Why did I get mixed up in this?"

"We'd do better to worry about getting out of it," Mabel replied. "Have you called Hudson?"

"No, I haven't. I wouldn't mind chewing him out, but I'd hate to ruin Addie's surprise."

"Call him at the church, then. You may catch him there."

Hudson arrived that afternoon and surveyed the two boxes in bewilderment. "I can't imagine what happened," he said. "I ordered just one Acme Queen Parlor organ. At least, I'm quite sure I did."

"Well, you now have two of them, Hudson. And my parlor is getting a bit cozy."

"I'm sorry, Sarah Jane. I'll send one back immediately. I didn't plan it this way."

"He couldn't jumble things up worse if he did plan them," Sarah Jane grumbled after he had left. "I certainly hope this is straightened out before Thomas gets home. He'd never let me forget it."

The excess organ was shipped back, and on the day that Thomas was due home, Hudson appeared in good time with one of his parishioners to pick up his crate. Sarah Jane gave a sigh of relief as the sleigh pulled out of sight and went about preparing for her husband's return.

Soon thereafter Thomas came through the door and dropped his valise on a chair.

"Ah, it's good to be home!" he said, hugging Sarah Jane affectionately. "I passed your old friend Hudson Curtis on the road with a huge load in his sleigh. Looked like he was on his way to the station."

Then his eyes twinkled merrily. "Speaking of large packages, do you have some news for me?" He headed for the parlor and then stopped at the threshold, looking about expectantly. "Where is it?" he asked in dismay.

"Where is what?" asked Sarah Jane. "If you're referring to Hudson Curtis's organ, though I don't know how you could be, it's in the back of his sleigh."

"What? Where's Hudson Curtis taking my organ? Wait until I catch him!"

Thomas ran toward the front door with Sarah Jane in hot pursuit.

"Thomas, whatever are you talking about? That was Hudson's organ! He asked if we'd store it for him till Christmas, so he could surprise Addie."

"That's not Hudson's organ, it's your organ! Didn't it have your name on it?"

"Actually, there were two organs here. Hudson sent the other one back."

By this time Thomas was fairly beside himself. "What?! Hudson sent my organ back? Why would he do a thing like that? That was your Christmas present!"

Sarah Jane and Thomas finally calmed down enough to sort out the mix-up, but Thomas wasn't pleased to find that his wife's wonderful Christmas surprise had come to town and left again without her even opening it.

On Christmas Day, Mabel and Len and their children sat in the Charleses' parlor with their friends, singing carols—without organ accompaniment. Thomas looked a bit glum, but Sarah Jane laughed.

"I'm sure we'll laugh about this for years to come," she said, "though Thomas certainly doesn't think it's funny. Oh, Mabel, do you think we'll ever learn to stay clear of Hudson Curtis?"

Thomas smiled wryly at his wife. "I'm not sure we can place all the blame on poor old Hudson this time. It took a whole team of experts to create this much Christmas confusion!"

Clare's Christmas Faith

*W*inter descended with a vengeance upon North Branch at the end of October. Snow lay on the ground, and frigid air rushed down from Canada. Suddenly it didn't seem too soon for the Williamses to think about Christmas.

In November Clare came home with exciting news.

"Sam and I have a job after school and on Saturdays!" he announced.

"A job! Clare, you're only seven years old!" Mabel glanced at Len in amusement.

"Almost eight," he corrected Mama. He looked at his father imploringly. "I can do it, can't I, Papa? I'll earn money for Christmas presents, and I'll share it with you."

"It depends on what the job is, son," Len replied. "And upon who is offering it to you. Is it someone we know?"

Clare nodded. "It's Mr. Gage at the store. He says that Sam and I can run errands and make deliveries and sweep out for him. I'm big enough to do that."

Len and Mabel agreed that Clare might try the job, and for the rest of the month, he came home happily each evening and added his pennies, and an occasional nickel, to the box where he kept his earnings.

"What are you going to do with all that wealth?" Mabel asked one afternoon. "You are collecting quite a bit there."

Clare beamed. "I haven't added on today's, but yesterday I already had thirty-four cents. I'll tell you a secret, if you promise not to tell."

"I promise."

"I'm going to get Papa a watch for Christmas!"

"A watch! My, what a wonderful gift!" Mabel tried to sound enthusiastic, but her heart dropped at the thought of the little boy's disappointment when he discovered that his resources would never cover anything so grand.

"There is one at Jackson's Jewelry Store that I have my eye on," Clare continued importantly. "Mr. Jackson says it is a very good watch, and he will hold it for me. You won't tell Papa, will you?"

Mabel promised again that she would not, but she did talk to Sarah Jane about it.

"There are only three weeks left until Christmas," she said. "What can I do for him when he tries to buy that watch for fifty cents?"

"Did you mention how much it probably would cost?" asked Sarah Jane.

"Yes. I also suggested that he might not make that much more before Christmas. When Len reminded him that the Lord's tithe needs to come out before he purchases his Christmas presents, I thought for sure Clare would give up his idea."

"But that didn't discourage him, huh? I suppose this is one of the lessons he'll have to learn from experience. That's tough for a little boy."

"That's not the worst part," Mabel sighed. "He told me not to worry about it, because he was praying for the watch every night."

"Your hands are tied," Sarah Jane said. "It's going to be

interesting to see how God handles this one."

"Interesting" was not the word Mabel chose when the week before Christmas arrived and Clare dumped his money on the bed for a final counting.

"I'll wait until the day before Christmas to pick up the watch," he said. "Or maybe the twenty-third. I might not make much more on the last day." His coins amounted to forty-eight cents.

"How much is a tenth of that?" he wanted to know.

"Four point eight cents," Mabel told him. "Almost five cents."

"The Lord deserves five cents for helping me," Clare said. "Besides, I don't know how much 'point eight' is."

"Am I being cruel in letting him believe that he'll get that watch?" Mabel said to Sarah Jane. "I wouldn't destroy his faith for anything in the world, but I don't know how I'll handle his disappointment."

"Mabel, the Lord honors faith wherever He finds it," Sarah Jane said. "Doesn't the Bible say that's what Jesus will look for when He returns to the earth?"

"Yes," Mabel nodded, "and it also says that faith is the 'evidence of things not seen.' That watch certainly qualifies."

On the twenty-third of December, Len came home with news.

"I had to make a trip into town this afternoon," he said, "and I'm afraid that the information I got isn't going to add to your Christmas spirit."

Mabel waited for him to continue.

"I was walking past the jewelry store when Mr. Jackson stepped out and asked to speak to me."

Oh, dear, Mabel thought. *He knows about the watch.*

Len cleared his throat and went on. "It seems that Clare has something that doesn't belong to him."

"You mean Mr. Jackson accused Clare of stealing?!" Mabel exclaimed. "How could he think such a thing? Clare is just a baby!"

"No, no, nothing like that," Len hastily replied. "Sit down, and I'll tell you the whole story. Or at least as much as I know. Mr. Jackson said that Clare came into the store a while ago to make a purchase, and emptied his pockets to pay for it. There were a number of pennies and some nickles, and in the midst of the coins was this."

Len opened his hand and set a small object on the table. Mabel gasped as the light struck and shimmered off a brilliant red stone.

"Oh, Len! What is it?"

"I didn't know, either," Len said. "Mr. Jackson says it is a fire opal. And a very expensive one."

"But where would Clare get such a thing?"

"That is what Mr. Jackson suggested we find out," Len replied. "Clare told him that a man at the hotel had given it to him. Clare said Mr. Jackson could have it along with the money, because it wasn't a very good marble."

"Oh, Len. What will we do now? I'm going to be nervous having that in the house."

"We'll straighten it out as soon as Clare comes home," Len soothed her. "I'm sure there's a reasonable explanation."

"I'm not," Mabel said. "I knew I should have just told Clare that there was no possible way he could afford—"

At that moment Clare burst through the door. When he saw the opal on the table, he stopped short.

"Where did you get the stone?"

"Mr. Jackson gave it to me, son," Len answered.

Clare looked at his mother accusingly. "Mama!" he wailed. "You promised you wouldn't say anything! You spoiled the surprise!"

Mabel shook her head, and Len spoke up.

"Your mama didn't tell me anything, Clare. Mr. Jackson told me you left this with him."

He pulled the little boy over to him and put his arm around him.

"Can you tell us where you got it?"

Clare was visibly relieved. "Sure. I was going by the hotel, and this man called me over and asked if I'd take a telegram to the telegraph office for him. I said sure, and he gave me that stone for my trouble." Clare poked it with his finger. "I guess he thought it was a marble, but anyone can see you couldn't shoot with it. Did Mr. Jackson say I could have it back?"

"Well, not exactly." Len said. "But he did think we'd better find out where it came from. Would you know the man if you saw him again?"

Clare nodded. He and Len returned to the hotel, only to find that the gentleman had checked out and presumably left on the evening train. There was nothing to do but keep the gem overnight. Mabel wrapped it carefully and hid it in the flour bin.

When Len returned to the jewelry store the next morning, Mr. Jackson met him with excitement.

"We know where the opal came from, Mr. Williams. It was stolen from a dealer in Detroit. The fellow evidently realized that they were closing in on him, and gave the stone to your son in the hope that he could reclaim it later. He must have panicked and got out while he still could. The good news is that there is a reward for its recovery!"

Len placed the stone on the counter. "What is the reward?" he asked cautiously.

"One hundred dollars," Mr. Jackson replied. He beamed happily. "Just in time for Christmas. You can finish your shopping in style."

Len stared at him in disbelief. "You mean that Clare will receive one hundred dollars? We've never had that much money at one time. We've never needed that much money. Clare can spend what he's earned on Christmas gifts, but this will go into the bank for him. I can't believe this."

"Oh, he's spent what he earned, all right," Mr. Jackson said with a chuckle, "and I'll see that he gets a fine . . . er . . . one. You have a great boy there, Mr. Williams. I like to see a boy with ambition. This was a lucky coincidence for him."

"No," Mabel said when Len repeated the conversation to her. "It wasn't a coincidence. I believe this is a response to Clare's faith. He prayed for enough to get a special gift for you, and he worked as hard as he could to earn it. The Lord always gives more than we can ask or think."

Christmas was a day of celebration. Clare proudly presented his papa with a watch which clearly cost more than the fifty-two cents he had earned for it, but Mr. Jackson had insisted that Clare did indeed pay for the gift.

"Christmas needs to be celebrated with peace, joy, and faith," Mabel said to Sarah Jane as they fixed turkey sandwiches for supper that evening. "I'm ashamed when I think of the hours I spent agonizing over Clare's disappointment instead of trusting the Lord to work things out. But you'll have to admit that it could have gone differently. What might have happened to his faith if it hadn't worked out this way? He really didn't earn enough for a watch."

"Clare will learn that life doesn't always hand out happy experiences," Sarah Jane replied, "but this Christmas will help him learn to trust the Lord. That won't desert him even when hard times come later. We discover something new every Christmas, don't we? No wonder it's such a special day of the year!"

Grandma and I were baking cookies for Christmas on a snowy Saturday morning.

"You've had a lot of Christmases, haven't you, Grandma?" I said. "Do you remember all of them?"

"Not in detail, Arleta," Grandma replied. "But I can recall many little separate incidents. I seem to remember the earlier ones better than the later years. What is the first Christmas you can remember?"

I thought for a moment. "I remember the year Aunt Claribel gave me Onalee," I said. "How old was I then?"

"Almost two," Grandma said. "I'm surprised you recollect that far back."

"I really don't remember anything except how much I loved that doll," I told her. "I wish I still had her."

"You were lucky to have her as long as you did," Grandma said with a chuckle. "I guess you never heard the whole of Onalee's story."

"No, but I'd like to. What happened?"

Grandma pushed a pan of cookies into the oven and sat down at the kitchen table to tell the story.

Onalee

𝓕rom the time you were a year old, you'd had your eye on Onalee. She had a cloth body and porcelain head and cried "Mama" when she was tipped over. Claribel was ten years older, and even though she didn't play with dolls much any more, she wasn't ready to give up that particular doll.

"Arleta's too little to have Onalee, Mama," Claribel said. "She'll just tear her apart."

"Well, you certainly don't have to give her the doll," I said.

Mabel's sister, Violet, was born when Mabel was twenty, and was just a few years older than Mabel's own daughter Alma. Alma's daughter, Arleta, spent part of her childhood in Grandma Mabel's care, and her Aunt Claribel (Mabel's third child, ten years younger than Alma and ten years older than Arleta) was like a big sister to the little girl.

"She has playthings of her own."

But Claribel was softhearted when it came to her only niece, so she would occasionally let you hold Onalee—as long as she was there to keep a sharp eye on the scene.

One day shortly before Christmas, Claribel came in from school and looked around the room.

"Where's Arleta?"

"In her room," I replied.

"She's still asleep this late?" Claribel asked.

"I don't think she's asleep," I said. "She's being punished. I told her she could stay there until she was ready to say 'please' when she asked for something."

"Can I try to get her to say it?"

"You can try. She got up this morning with a stubborn streak."

Claribel went in to persuade you, but all her coaxing was to no avail. When dinnertime came and you had not changed your mind, Claribel became desperate. She made one more trip to the bedroom and very shortly came back, leading you by the hand.

"She's ready to say please, Mama."

You did so, and you were allowed back into the good graces of the family.

Aunt Violet drew Claribel aside. "However did you manage that?" she asked.

"I promised her she could have Onalee for Christmas," Claribel said. "She'll probably forget about it before then."

If anyone believed that, they were in for a surprise. Not only did you remember, you made sure everyone else in the house did, too.

"It's a good thing you didn't promise her that doll in June," Aunt Violet said. "I'd have moved out of here months ago."

On Christmas morning Onalee was turned over to you, and from that moment the doll never left your sight. Onalee was squeezed and pulled around the house by an arm or leg. Of course it wasn't long before the poor doll began to separate at the seams.

This was of no concern to you, but the rest of the family soon tired of cleaning up the trail of white stuff that stuck to the furniture and carpets. It was especially annoying to Aunt Violet,

who followed you and Onalee around, picking at the chairs and rugs.

One day Aunt Violet reached the limits of her endurance.

"Just as soon as Arleta goes down for her nap," she announced, "I'm going to get rid of that pesky doll. I'll just go out and buy her another one."

True to her word, Aunt Violet removed Onalee from your bed and proceeded to the basement to deposit the doll in the furnace.

A short time later, Aunt Violet was observed with cotton batting, needle and thread, and what appeared to be Onalee on her lap.

"I thought you were going to burn that doll," I said.

"So did I," Aunt Violet replied, "but when I went to toss her into the furnace, she cried. I couldn't do it."

> *"So Onalee had a long, happy life,"*
> *Grandma concluded. "It's no wonder*
> *you've always loved dolls so much." She*
> *smiled fondly at me. "It runs in the*
> *family!"*

Field Day

Mabel tells of a Christmas adventure with four-year-old granddaughter Arleta.

$\mathcal{T}$he Christmas of 1927 was very different indeed from any I had ever known. Aside from the fact that it was the first time Sarah Jane and I had not been together for at least part of the day, Chicago was not at all like North Branch!

That big city was the last place I had ever expected to be, but in November a letter had arrived from Alma.

Mama, do you think you could come and stay with us? Harry and I are both so busy that we haven't the time to spend with Arleta. The housekeeper, Emma, is very good to her, but now that Arleta is four, she should have more personal attention. What she really needs is a grandma.

So the week before Christmas found me looking out over Lake Michigan from the big apartment window.

"I'm glad to have water out here," I said to Alma. "It reminds me of my Chippewa River, even if I can't see across it."

"You can hardly even see it this morning," she said. "The sky and the lake are the same color."

She looked over my shoulder at the snow coming down. "You aren't going to try to go out today, are you? It's going to be awfully windy and cold."

"I grew up in more snow and cold than this, Alma, and so did you," I told her. "I couldn't disappoint Arleta. She's looking forward to seeing the decorations downtown."

"You've never gone around town by yourself, Mama. I'd worry about you finding your way alone."

I assured her that we would stay in one place until they came to pick us up.

"After all, how could we possibly get lost in Marshall Field's?" I said. Then I laughed.

"What's so funny, Mama?"

"For a moment I thought I heard Sarah Jane saying, 'Be careful, Mabel—you're tempting fate!' We learned never to say 'What could possibly happen?' "

It was decided that Arleta and I would go directly to the big department store, and Harry would come to get us in the afternoon. Alma wrapped her fur coat around her and pulled on her gloves.

"If you're sure you'll be all right, then. . . . Have a nice time. Let Emma call a cab for you, and Harry will pick you up at three o'clock. And for goodness' sake, don't carry packages. Have them sent out. Let someone do something for you for a change."

She started for the door, then turned around again. "Are you sure you don't want Emma to go with you?"

"Of course not. She has her work to do. Now go, and don't worry about us."

I'll admit that I would have appreciated a familiar face when the cab driver set us down at the entrance to Marshall Field's. A four year old is a lot of fun, but not much help in a crisis.

"Now don't let go of Grandma's hand," I warned her. "If you get lost in all this mob, I'll never find you again."

Cars whizzed by, and elevated trains clattered overhead. People were clutching their coats to keep from having them whipped off in the wind. I had to use both hands to open my purse and pay the driver, and in that instant Arleta was gone! I must have looked pretty frantic, because the driver quickly reassured me.

"Don't worry, ma'am. She isn't going far."

He pointed at the big store window where Arleta stood with her nose pressed against the glass.

"Oh, Grandma! Look! Here's Santa and all the elves," Arleta squealed.

I was as fascinated by the scene as she was. Santa nodded his head as he watched small hammers pounding, needle and thread going in and out, toy dogs barking, and dolls dancing. Little boy and girl mannequins skated around on a pond of ice. It was too much to absorb all at once.

Finally I said, "We'd better go inside. It's getting colder. We'll look again when we come out to wait for your father."

Arleta pushed into a space with me in the revolving door.

"I don't like this," she said. "I'm afraid it won't let me out."

I didn't admit that I wasn't comfortable with it either, but I was glad that the doorman held the door for us when we got inside.

The warm air felt good after the icy blast outdoors. We stopped to look around with awe at the gorgeous decorations all over the store. The big tree that stood in the center of the floor sparkled with silver and lights, and was decorated with balls that glittered and shone.

My mind went back to a very different tree that once stood in a little country schoolhouse.

Oh, look, Ma! isn't it beautiful? Our grade made the paper chains to put on it. Roy's grade did the popcorn balls. Did you ever see a prettier tree?

A tug on my sleeve reminded me that Arleta was anxious to start her shopping.

"First a present for Emma," she said. "Something red. That's her favorite color."

After some discussion we selected a scarf and gloves, and Arleta took the money from her little purse to pay for them.

"Now we get to see the money fly," she informed me. We watched the clerk put the bill into a little cylindrical case, which she placed in a wire basket.

"There it goes!" The basket whizzed up to a room above the main floor, where the change was put in the case and sent back to our clerk.

Now that we had seen this wonder performed, it was time to visit Santa.

"Toyland is on the third floor, madam," the floor walker directed. He pointed the way to the escalator and elevator.

Arleta looked at me anxiously. "Do you want to go up the escalator, Grandma?"

"I think I prefer the elevator," I replied, and by the relieved look on her face, I knew I'd chosen wisely.

It took some persuasion to get Arleta on the back of the pony to have her picture taken with Santa.

"He's not going to run away with you," I assured her. "I used to ride ponies like this, and they are very gentle."

She consented to being lifted up, but I could tell that she would be glad when she was safely on the floor again.

As I watched Santa talking to the apprehensive little girl, I could hear another voice from the past.

"Have you been a good girl this year?"

I nodded, hoping that Santa Claus hadn't heard about the times I had been something less than perfect.

"Then there must be a package here for you."

I waited breathlessly until a gift was placed in my hands. No matter that Roy said Ma bought the gift. It came from Santa.

We looked at all of the toys in the department, and what a wonderland it was! I could never have imagined having all these things to play with. We lingered the longest at the display of dolls.

"There's the one Santa will bring me." Arleta pointed to a beautiful doll with long curls, real eyelashes, and eyes that moved. "I'm going to call her Rosemary. Isn't that a pretty name?"

I nodded, but I was back in our old kitchen.

An old rag doll, stuffed with popcorn, lay on the back of the stove to dry out.

"I'm going to name her Charlotte, Ma. Don't you think that's a pretty name?"

Did it matter whether it was Rosemary, with a twenty-five dollar price tag, or Charlotte, rescued from a mud puddle, as long as the small mother loved it?

"I'm hungry, Grandma."

"All right. Let's go wash up for lunch."

The ladies' lounge, with gleaming white tile, was decorated for Christmas, too. A small tree stood in the corner, and colored lights surrounded the mirrors. I chuckled to myself as I searched in my bag for a nickel. Imagine paying to open the bathroom door! I'm surprised one of my brothers didn't think of that, if for no other reason than to torment his little sister!

It felt good to sit down in the tea room. I realized that I was getting hungry, too.

"I want a peanut butter sandwich," Arleta announced.

I scanned the menu. "I don't see any peanut butter here. Wouldn't a nice chicken salad taste good?"

The additional promise of ice cream for dessert brought a reluctant agreement, and we settled back to eating lunch.

"Will we finish shopping after we eat, Grandma?"

"Yes," I replied. "We need to find something nice for your mother and daddy."

"And for you, Grandma! Something for you. You'll have to turn around while I buy it, so it will be a surprise."

By the time we had finished our shopping I was thankful that Alma had insisted that I have the packages sent home. When it was almost three o'clock, we started back to the door to wait for Harry.

"Grandma," Arleta reminded me, "you said we could see the window again when we came back out. Can we go look until Daddy comes?"

I had promised, all right, so we went out the big doors onto the cold, windy street. It was still noisy and windy and cold, but as far as I could see, that was all that was the same. There was no toyland in the window, no mannequins skating, no Santa "ho-ho-" ing.

"Grandma, this isn't the window we saw before."

"I see that," I said.

"What happened to it?" Arleta asked.

"I'm sure it's right where it was this morning," I told her. "We are the ones who are in the wrong place. We'd better go back in and find out where we are."

The doorman was most helpful. "Yes, ma'am. There is an entrance on Madison. You are at the State Street entrance."

He pointed us in the right direction, and I hurried off across the store. By now it was past three o'clock, and I was afraid we had missed Harry.

"Daddy will find us," Arleta assured me. "We can look at the toy window while we wait."

Looking up and down the busy street, I wasn't too sure about that. The cab had let us off at the store, but how did I know which was considered the "front" entrance?

Somewhere I've heard that if you stand in one place long enough, everyone you've ever known will pass by. When four o'clock came and went, I had seen hundreds of people, none of whom had gone by before, as far as I could tell. We had gone around in the revolving door so often that the doorman seemed like an old friend. Finally he had a suggestion.

"Madam, let me get a cab for you. Go on back home. Your son-in-law will check for you there, I'm sure."

This seemed to be a sensible solution. It was after dark when we arrived back at the apartment, and Alma was pacing the floor.

"Mama! Where on earth have you been? Did you get lost?"

"Of course not," I said. "I knew right where we were. I just didn't know where Harry was."

Alma helped me out of my coat and boots, and Emma took Arleta off to be fed and put to bed.

"Harry came home at three-thirty. He waited at the entrance for twenty minutes, then decided you'd gotten tired and taken a cab home. When he didn't find you here, he went right back to look for you. He's called every fifteen minutes to see if I've heard from you."

"Oh, my, what a bother," I said. "I just didn't know that the store had two front doors. We were standing at one of them while Harry was at the other."

Alma and Harry were so relieved to have us home safely

that neither one of them thought to ask me why I hadn't called home. So I didn't have to tell them that I'd never used a telephone that didn't have an operator to talk to. As I wrote a letter to Sarah Jane that evening, I thought of the many holidays we had spent together over the years.

I suppose I would get used to all this if I lived in the city long enough, but I believe North Branch is more to my liking. I know I shall miss you and Thomas on Christmas Day.

Give my love to your family, and rest assured that the big city has not changed your old friend. My heart is still in the country and, I suspect, always will be. . . .

Aunt Beat's Forgotten Christmas

*T*here are two days of the year that no one ever forgets—her birthday and Christmas. Right? If you think so, you reckon without my great-aunt Beat.

I suppose every family has at least one eccentric member. Without question, Grandma's brother's widow was ours. Aunt Beat was fiercely independent. Although she happily joined the family for holidays and parties, she lived alone. Her son insisted that she install a telephone, but she usually refused to answer it. He provided electricity, which she also ignored. Since she no longer kept a horse, she walked wherever she wanted to go.

My Uncle Roy was openly annoyed with Aunt Beatrice. Grandma was more tolerant. Aunt Violet allowed as how she just might get that way herself if she lived long enough. (She did.) But to me, Aunt Beat was a continuing wonder.

Christmas was Aunt Beat's favorite holiday. Back in the days when one never saw a decorated tree until Christmas morning, Aunt Beat began celebrating the occasion months ahead of time. Suddenly, without any advance notice, she would shout, "Do you know how many days are left until Christmas?"

If I happened to be the one she asked, along about the middle of May, I always had to confess that I had absolutely no idea.

"I'm not surprised, Arleta," she would say. "Just like your grandmother. Always have your face in a book. You need to keep up with these things."

So no one was prepared for what happened the Christmas I was ten.

After the church service on this particular Christmas Eve, Grandma suggested that Beatrice stay overnight with us. "So we can get a nice early start in the morning," Grandma explained.

To no one's surprise, the offer was refused.

"Can't do that. Have chores to do and pies to bake yet tonight. I'll be there before daylight tomorrow."

"You can count on that," Uncle Roy muttered. "Sure as death and taxes."

Christmas morning came, and I was allowed out of bed as soon as the kitchen was warm. Grandma and my Uncle Roy's wife, Aunt Celia, were the only ones about.

"Where's Aunt Beat?" I asked.

"It's early yet," Grandma replied. "She'll be along directly."

Uncle Roy came in. "It's almost six o'clock. Where's the Christmas trumpet?"

"We'll go ahead and start breakfast," Aunt Celia said, ignoring the comment. "She'll be here any minute."

According to our custom, I could open stocking gifts right away, but the other presents had to wait until after breakfast. When Aunt Beat failed to appear while we ate, I began to suspect that things might be delayed even longer, and I kept a watchful eye on the door. Grandma, too, made several trips to the window, although it was still too dark to see past the porch.

"I can't imagine what's keeping her," Grandma said. "Do you think we'd better call?"

Uncle Roy calmly proceeded with his breakfast.

"Save your strength. Even if she weren't as deaf as a

doorknob, she'd still be too stubborn to answer the telephone. Beatrice dances to her own music."

We all knew this was true; nevertheless, when Aunt Beat had not come by the time breakfast was cleared away, Aunt Violet roused Flora, the town watchperson and telephone operator.

"Flora, is there any light at Beat's house?"

There was a pause while Flora went to look.

"Then ring her for me, will you, please?"

Another long pause.

"Well, all right. I know she doesn't, but try every once in a while anyway, and let us know if you get her."

The morning wore on, and the ladies began preparations for Christmas dinner. I played a half-hearted game of checkers with Uncle Roy. He wasn't about to admit it, but he was growing increasingly uneasy himself.

"Mabel," he called at last. "This child is beginning to look pathetic. At least let her open a couple of packages. Who knows when that woman will get here?"

At that moment the telephone rang, and Uncle Roy leaped to get it. It was Flora.

"Lettie says that Jake thinks he saw Beat's boy's car out here this morning," she reported. "So she guesses that like as not he took his mother with him."

"I doubt that," Aunt Celia said when the news was passed on to us. "It's not like Beatrice to go off without letting us know."

"Hah!" Uncle Roy snorted. "Sounds just like something she'd do, if you ask me."

"Well, I'm not easy in my mind," Aunt Celia insisted. "I'd feel better if you just went on over there and checked out the house."

Uncle Roy grumbled as he buckled on his galoshes and wrapped his scarf around his neck. Since it looked like neither presents nor dinner would be forthcoming until the matter was settled, I bundled up and went with him.

I sat in the old car while Uncle Roy thrashed the front door, the back door, and all the windows he could reach. After a couple of turns around the house, he came back to the car.

"I told Celia this would be a fool trip. She's gone, all right."

The rest of the day passed uneventfully, and everyone agreed that an early bedtime was in order. Uncle Roy banked the fires, Aunt Celia said again what a pity it was that Beatrice hadn't been with us, and we retired.

It must have been close to three o'clock in the morning when a dreadful battering began on the front door. Uncle Roy's voice rose above the din.

"What in thunder is that? Who's there? Hold on. Don't bust the house down."

All the rest of us gathered on the steps as Uncle Roy flung open the door. Aunt Beat sailed in, her arms full of packages with a pie balanced on top. She stopped and eyed Uncle Roy with surprise.

"You still standing around here in your nightshirt?" she boomed. "I told you I'd be here before daylight."

She bustled off toward the kitchen, and her voice wafted back to us.

"Looks like I'll have to get the breakfast started while you get dressed. Can't imagine you oversleeping on Christmas Day. I worked late last night, and I managed to get around this morning."

We looked at each other in disbelief. Even Uncle Roy was speechless.

"She thinks today is Christmas," Grandma said. "Where in the world has she been?"

"I know where she is headed," Uncle Roy stated ominously. "Doesn't that confounded woman have a clock in her house? I'm going back to bed."

"You can't, Roy. Beatrice hasn't had any Christmas yet. We'll have to get dressed and come down and eat breakfast." Aunt Celia marched back up the stairs, and the rest of us followed.

"You mean we have to fix another Christmas dinner?" Aunt Violet asked. "And how are you going to break the news that we already opened our gifts without her?"

Of course no one had the answer to that. We dressed and sat down to breakfast, and as tactfully as possible, Grandma asked Aunt Beat where she'd been since the Christmas Eve service.

"Why, home in bed, of course. Where else would decent people be?"

"You mean you slept all day Christmas, Aunt Beat?" I asked.

"Certainly not!" she replied indignantly. "Why would I do a thing like that? T'aint even daylight yet. I was up before any of you were."

Uncle Roy pushed his chair back.

"Well, ladies," he said cheerfully, "I leave you to sort this one through. I'm going to stretch out on the sofa and catch a few more winks. Call me when it's time to open the presents."

He grinned broadly and disappeared.

It took some doing, but Aunt Beat finally admitted that she had been pretty tired, and that she might have slept through the day if she had been lying on her good ear . . . but she denied to her last breath that she had ever forgotten Christmas Day.

Grandma's Christmas Cake

*O*ne of the yearly customs in Grandma's house was the baking of the Christmas cake. This was a family affair, since everyone helped to crack and pick out the black walnuts. The children wrapped the coins that were folded into the batter at the last minute, to be discovered in nearly every piece of cake on Christmas Day and exchanged for candy or a small toy from the tree. (The coins were then put into a bank to be saved or spent later.)

The children were also allowed to arrange the gum drops on top of the cake in any way they chose, so the cake was decorated differently each year. I recall thumb prints that broke through the crispy top of the icing, but even with these—or perhaps because of them—the Christmas cake was the most beautiful creation of the year!

GRANDMA'S CHRISTMAS CAKE

3 cups sugar
1 cup butter
2 cups milk
5 cups cake flour
1 teaspoon vanilla
4 teaspoons baking powder
1/4 teaspoon salt
6 egg whites, beaten
2 cups cranberries, chopped
1 cup citron, chopped
1 cup black walnuts, chopped
coins wrapped in oiled paper

Beat the butter and sugar until very light and creamy. Add the milk alternately with four cups of the flour. Add vanilla and beat thoroughly. Sift baking powder and salt into the last cup of flour; add to batter. Add the well-beaten egg whites. Carefully fold in the cranberries, citron, black walnuts, and coins.

Bake about forty minutes in three 9-inch layers. This will make a large cake. Frost with boiled icing.

BOILED ICING

1 1/2 cups sugar
1/2 teaspoon light corn syrup
2/3 cup boiling water
2 egg whites, stiffly beaten
1 teaspoon vanilla

Combine sugar, corn syrup, and water. Bring quickly to a boil, stirring only until sugar is dissolved. Boil rapidly, without stirring, until small amount of syrup forms a soft ball in cold water. Pour syrup in fine stream over egg whites, beating constantly. Add vanilla. Continue beating 10 to 15 minutes, or until icing is cool and of right consistency to spread.

Frost cold cake and decorate with red and green gumdrops.

Ask for these Grandma's Attic Series
titles from Chariot Books